Copyright © 2023 Jamie H. Cowa

To The Smallest Grain Of Sand and all related characters are copyright © 2023 Jamie H. Cowan.

The right of Jamie H. Cowan to be identified as the author of this work is asserted by him in accordance with the Copyright, Designs and Patents Act 1988.

No part of this publication may be reproduced, stored in a retrieval system, or - in any form or by any means – otherwise circulated in any form of binding, cover or ebook other than which it is published, without the prior permission in writing of the publisher and the author. Any subsequent publisher or circulator cannot do so without a similar set of conditions being imposed upon their publication or circulation of the work.

This is a work of fiction. Names, places and incidents are either the product of the author's imagination; or if real, used in a fictitious manner. All material contained within this work is included for the purposes of entertainment and should not be relied upon for accuracy or replication – as they may result in injury or other negative circumstances or incorrect perceptions of reality.

First published 2023 by Overmorrow Publishing.

This edition published 2023 by Overmorrow Publishing.

Edited by Jeffrey Princeton.

Cover by Jamie H. Cowan.

THANKS

With thanks to:

Jeffrey Princeton - for his usual editorial duties.

Ryan Williams - for always believing in my mad but fun writing work.

Tom Frost - for keeping me sane daily in a way that few people ever can or have. You're one of the absolute best in the world.

Lynn - for reminding me to take some form of breaks amidst my busy days.

Campbell P. - for helping me see a brighter side of myself.

The many, many other people in this universe - who I have been friends of, cared about, lost, loved or otherwise emoted about.

My family - who have had to endure me scribbling away poetry, day and night, in the background of their lives.

Chris & Patrick – for some of the best writing insight I think I've ever had.

CONTENTS

Copyright
Thanks

Before the Shades

PROLOGUE

Shade of Purple 1: Friends

IN OUR BATTLEGROUND
TENNYSON'S TRUTH
HOW YOU WILL LOSE
BEGINS ANEW
RASPBERRY RIPPLE
GANG AFT AGLEY
ABOUT ANY OTHER WORLDS
ANOTOGETHER
YOUR MOMENT
FLOWERCHILD

Shade of Purple 2: Loss

WHEN LAID TO REST
MARNIE
CUDDLE
SUMMER REMINISCENCE
ICARUS
ONE BRONZE RING
GLASS
HOW I WISH YOU TO DO MY FUNERAL
FRAGMENTAL
MEMORY HOLE

Shade of Purple 3: The World Beyond

DECIPHER
BRICK WORK
UNTIMED
WORDS OF POWER
CONTRARY
YOUR FIRST RULE
HAIKU-SENRYŪ
LINES DRAWN
THE QUARTET
JOB'S WORTH

Shade of Purple 4: Stageplay

REGIMENT
DEMETRIUS 1
EXCERPT FROM A LETTER TO JEFFY
SEVEN AND FIVE
UPON MY NAME
MICHAEL
ON THE JOB
THE BARTENDER AND THE BODYGUARD
UNABRIDGED
A FINAL BOW

Shade of Purple 5: The World Inside

UNTITLED
LIVERPUDLIAN B&M
YOUR DAY TODAY
BRONZE, SILVER, GOLD
BEACH
TO BE
DAYS, NIGHTS
SANDS OF MIND
WILD BLUE YONDER
INAMORATO

Shade of Purple 6: Lust

THE APP
AS DONE UNDER NEON
ANOTHER FOLLY
GAME
WINE
CUFF LINKS
NAME UNSAID
UN/RAVEL
(S)WORDS
WORDS

Shade of Purple 7: Love

SWIPE
SWING
GENTLE COULD HAVE
TO BE SPOKEN ALOUD IN AN EMPTY ROOM
TAKE THE WORLD
SCENT
KNOW
CHERISH
EMMET'S FAINT WORDS
BEHIND BLUE EYES

After the Shades
EPILOGUE

About The Author

BEFORE THE SHADES

PROLOGUE

So many things that we are barely muttering
enveloped in a fear of uttering.
Words in the broadest sense
rather than shrugging off the pretense.

The universe in which we often feel unable
to impart the truth - lest we become unstable.
But the fear is simply an irrationality as
we fail to see that's what emotion often has.

Swear in joy and cry with laughter
whilst you think on happily about what comes after.
Lie in bed, think and stare
up - perhaps even, in frustration, swear.

Do not let the emotions hold you from your thought
and your truths and what should never be forgot.
So come all ye come, say what you will of existence
and tell people - make that your resistance.

Tell them their talents and their beauty and your love,
from the daybreak until you see stars above.

SHADE OF PURPLE 1: FRIENDS

IN OUR BATTLEGROUND

It's a time when it feels like we're losing it all,
But every second - our care seems to break the fall.

As it all shall collide and bring an end of days,
We're the team that always stays.

If caring about you all puts me in danger,
Then I'd rather that than be a safe stranger.

If caring about you all involves risks to be faced,
Then, into that challenge, I shall be placed.

I'd rather fight the battles with you all,
Than be tucked away alone, safe from the brawl.

In the near-apocalypse that we shall face,
We shall all be one another's safe place.

TENNYSON'S TRUTH

You feel so blue upon verse's call
When they speak makeshift remedy.
Yet I speak that they should recall
T'was not meant for lovers at all.

The man papered it in his engulfing loss
Not one of seeds often sown by two.
The man papered it for what a death costs
To that of a friend – yet we come to woo.

They speak their sight yet don't see the spoken
Of one's friend loved so dearly.
And they mistake in a cycle unbroken
How the duo were tied so clearly.

Love beyond passion and romance
That is the papered truth there to glance.
In simply a dear friend
For which the man had penned.

HOW YOU WILL LOSE

And you're trying to save me
From what I will be
But the last six that tried ended up
With their hearts broken
And stories to tell
At parties.

They have songs to write and poems to make
Of what it would take
But they will never have written them
For I opened to them
And they closed
Off.

This is how you will lose
Because I will, in the end, never be what you choose.

BEGINS ANEW

Darkness

Then

Flame ignite
Ray of light
A fresh new start
Under a change of heart
No pain defining our ways
As we move onto new days
With nothing around to hold us back
And no need to stay on that old beaten-up track.

Together - we overcome
And today, the revolution has begun.

RASPBERRY RIPPLE

(Written by me on April 18th 2018. Later re-worked and properly adapted by Chris McCafferty & me into a song of the same name.)

Heart of red,
Glass of wine.
Stuck in my head,
Breaking all sense of time.

I keep declaring
"Hey, I'm just fine."
But with what you're wearing,
It's no wonder I'm a broken rhyme.

Trying to keep focused,
Dying to stay happy.
Aim to see you - hear you call,
Life's a sadness - a slow crawl.

Abstinence's my committal,
To your heart of raspberry ripple.

I wish I could fight,
I wish I could hold on tight
But no point when it's not
What the world has sought.

Never get where I'm coming from,
Never really seeing me for me.
Tell me, how did I go to
Looking like I love you?

Black hair blowing in that wind,
Your eyes entice me in,
That charming smile you wear so well,
This feels so good, feels so bad.
All of you can do me wrong.

I don't think I can say,
How you make me feel this way.
My heart melts away to red...
Why can't yours instead?

Abstinence's my committal,
To your heart of raspberry ripple.

GANG AFT AGLEY

A wee bit o' a trouble
Maybee just nought to be
Cast an e'e o'er what thou scribe
An' tell ye that the words are awfy well-done.

But there's nothing promis'd in
My words for ye cannae seem to find
Just how wonderful ye have been
In my distanc'd gushing words.

ABOUT ANY OTHER WORLDS

In any other world
Of which it can be said
That I know
Nothing.

I would certainly hope
That you and I were with
All the
Others.

For you are all the
Things that came into
My humble little
Universe.

And what could ever be
The point in worrying about
Another time that isn't
Mine?

Absent of all the stars
That are my friends within
Our own glimmering
Constellation.

As our planet turns in
Our world and time
We move through the skies
Together.

And the promise of the Omniverse
Fails to compell me compared to the
Simple pleasures of our quaint
Unity.

ANOTOGETHER

Shuffling to and fro,
Hard to breathe,
Though I'd never leave,
You to alone go.

We toss and turn in the frustrations of,
The life we've been thrust into,
We're bound together in the glue,
Of a certain kind of love.

Even out where the air is cold,
Or the sweat clings to my clothes,
You're all the team that I chose,
To stick by as I grow old.

Another day is where I belong,
When it comes to this little crowd,
In moments together quiet and loud,
So come, team, come along.

YOUR MOMENT

This is the moment
Now is the time.
Here is the poem
Thus to rhyme.

You can hear a tale
And maybe resonate with your story.
If there is even but a glimmering
Chord of truth - 'tis a victory.

Perhaps here is where you, my friend, can help
Give your own resonance that you will remember.
Remember that this will have been
The piece of art of which you were a member.

The iridescent key to the meaning of
_____.
It's never anything but the sparkled
_____.

FLOWERCHILD

When you went away,
I seemed to have a lot less to say.

Never should I have taken it all for granted,
Your absence leaves me disenchanted.

Knowing people was the best part,
Of living for my heart.

But now, I am left wrecked,
Shards of emotions to collect.

There is all that I never got to do or say,
Because I never thought you'd go away.

The tie I never got to buy you,
For all the flowers wilt - and I go blue.

SHADE OF PURPLE 2: LOSS

WHEN LAID TO REST

Do we call death the blackness
Such that we do not have to picture?
Is the blindfold taken to avoid
Sight of bullet, illness, fire, end?

We confine the dying and the dead,
To mortuary and to hospital bed.
Some even fall to rest,
In the care homes afar.

When we take the body home,
If it be taken at all,
We box it in so that we never consider
The entirety of what has gone.

Often, they are suited in their Sunday best
As though merely sleeping,
For a day of work ahead
Instead of what is plainly true.

We content ourselves with the silence
Of a light gentle going through the night,
In a falsity of glamour
As though death might be so often given.

We hid our bones and decay
Behind a curtain,
Alongside the stage managers
Of the funeral homes.

Whilst Japan pick up their beloved bones
And place them in their urns,
The Tibetans leave their bodies not buried
But to the animals as generous return.

Some will bury where others will burn,
Farewell for months when some - just day one.
The Muslims must burn their bodies,
Less than a day after they left.

The world forever in a cycle of being bereft,
But that cycle shifts ever more.
Where once mourners wore white,
We have put upon them robes of black.

Remember - let the bodies not lack,
An Obol to help pay Charon back.
Yet still, the Vietnamese would urge you send
Their dying home for else would bring bad luck.

Perhaps with some here, a chord may be struck,
But then who am I to duck?
There is plenty upon which I am stuck,
As I try to swim from the seas we've built.

For myself, however, I feel a touch of guilt,
For when my loved ones continue to wilt...
What can I do once the sands of time be spilt?
How can our seeing of the end be rebuilt?

Some fast, some at a slow speed,
In elder years or in far too soons.
And all the in-between,
That remains to be seen.

When days come that I must tend to my father,
I feel we will equal tears with the laughter.
But I will only know when the time come,
For the road to that inevitable outcome.

And when the days come to tend my mother,
I suspect she will wish to go fighting.
Never would I begrudge her that but,
I have no say in when Chronos makes that final cut.

Will I call death the blackness
Such that I do not have to picture?
Will I take a blindfold to avoid
Sight of bullet, illness, fire, end?

MARNIE

Marnie, oh Marnie
Why do you hide?
Marnie, oh Marnie
Time for your life.

Turning from slumber
Awake to a crumbling place
Knowing too well a breakneck pace.

Under those skies, you cannot disguise
You've got to run on lands most unwise
Running across the hills of old Druimblaire
Avoiding the pain of smoky spectre's glare.

Marnie, oh Marnie
With the creak of my bones do I hate
Marnie, oh Marnie
That you're trapped into this fate.

Take a stand
And make for a plan
Even as you go back to where it began.

Bagpipes clamour
As shadows cross the castles
And the smith should drop hammer
At the fleeing of the vassals
Marnie, oh Marnie
We've lost our flowers and steeds
Marnie, oh Marnie
They come to wreck havoc with misdeeds.

Running and spinning
The world needs you winning
With that battered old shoebox in your hand.

When living and living and living meets
That old formal death in the streets
It meets the unforgiving time
To that date you're resigned.
Marnie, oh Marnie.

CUDDLE

Julian misses the night
Where he got to cuddle
You.

When you both lay in that
Bed together amidst the dark
Night-time.

And he tentatively wrapped his
Arms around you as though
Instinct.

It felt to Julian as though he'd
Never really known before just what
A hug was.

When the sun rose, he didn't
Want to let go as you both
Lay at rest.

Knowing that you felt like a
Perfect fit
In-between his chest and his arms.

Feeling his heart beat so close
To yours, and knowing that
It was like a whole new emotion itself.

But then, the alarm came
And slowly you slipped from Julian's arms
Leaving him resigned to fate.

The emptiness of his arms jagging
Like some loose tooth at the back of his mouth
That would never go away.

Julian feels the absence of you in
Every morning since
And every night to come.

All he's ever wishing for
Is to get you back in his arms
For even just one more minute.

SUMMER REMINISCENCE

Let us not pretend
that you are still my friend.
I have no doubts
we've gone on our divergent routes.

There are no small talks
or late-night streetlight-lit walks.
For I am Miguel
and yet you no longer dwell.

Running down those narrow streets
listening to all the rumbling beats.
The prominent summer tune
underscoring our antics at noon.

I remember all that of the past, yet
in the present - I am something you forget.
And I know not that in the forthcoming
times that I will be alone amidst the drumming.

ICARUS

Icarus has flown
too close to the
Sun.

Icarus has known
those wings are gonna
burn.

Icarus has thrown
it all away because he didn't
learn.

Icarus has sewn
an end for all that he did
yearn.

Icarus has never known
that his father has given him this fate to
earn.

ONE BRONZE RING

It was a ring I found in Aviemore
That young me happened to adore.
Going along the path I had seen
This thing amongst the grassy green.

A humble little thing
Because what else would be a bronze ring?
So, with no return to be made
I decided that - with me - it stayed.

When first made, in gold paint it had been dipped
But when I found it - 'twas long since mostly chipped.
I think it was back in two thousand and eleven
When I took through the forest with tree of heaven.

At any rate, it was worn so often through my
schooldays That more of the faint gold would graze.
It stayed upon my hand plenty other times
From morning starts to midnight chimes.

Then I - like its past owner - came to lose
This ring that I had decided to choose.
It was in early two thousand and eighteen
When I took it off for a scene.

In the town hall at night
Auditioning with all my might.
I removed it and slipped into my coat
As it was not part of the words that I had to quote.

The rare times were the parts I played
Where, on my hand, the ring had not stayed.
After I had given the audition one hundred percent
I lifted my coat and off I went.

It was only later that I realised the absence
And I have not forgotten since.
The staff were unable to help the next day
And none of my friends had anything helpful to say.

I am sure that one could replace
With a ring identical on face.
But some easily bought novelty
Would not fit any kind of honesty.

Even now, I wonder who came to find
That ring that was one of a kind.
Not of any pretending youthful gold
But instead an honest bronzing old.

The ring that once, into my life, spun
And before that, belonged to another someone.
The bronze leaf ring that went so many places
On my hand as I greeted so many faces.

A ring like it, I will never have again
For there are some things you cannot feign.
In all the years for it - I will especially miss
That ring, 'twas on my hand when I'd my very first kiss.

GLASS

In my room,
Stationary,
There for some time,
When the window opened.

The wind rushes in,
And over me,
As brown eyes,
Gaze in the glass.

Eyes beginning for a move,
A step to be taken,
Amidst a look,
Of sorrow.

It's a reflection,
But what is that expression?
Why does it beg me so,
To turn and go?

HOW I WISH YOU TO DO MY FUNERAL

Mourn me not with the sharpest black.
Come in the brightest of hues,
To celebrate the vibrance of when I was here,
Rather than some grim wish to have me back.

I know that you might happen to miss me.
So, share round the stories and the photos,
Even the rock & musical playlists of shows gone,
For that's the picture of me for you all to see.

Do not box me up, for that's not how I should be found.
Let me dressed in a fitting shirt and purple sweater,
Then be wrapped in some simple humble robe,
All to be lowered into the ground.

Let the trumpets play as excitedly as normal.
Sing all the songs in cheerful merriment,
As you think of me,
Personally but not formal.

There be speeches to happen.
I would hope in those that,
There might be found some in-jokes,
And definitely a pun.

That is how it should be done.
It's my funeral, after all,
And, barring serious accidents,
I'll only get the one.

Do not take this away from me - this idle will.
Let the day end not in some little pub,
Quietly sharing stories of me but instead,
Conjure up a party to commemorate life's thrill.

Dance in all your colours across the floor.
Finding smiles even as your tears fall,
Because life is more than one emotion at a time,
And I know which I wish you to keep at your core.

Lead my body out of the funeral by no song.
Instead, think of me and cheer,
For the care and love of all expressed,
Is a send-off that will do no wrong.

Let all present believe what they will of my fate.
Give everyone their space and moment to think,
Of the past and what they see to be my future,
As I am so distinctly late.

On these proceedings, please no scorn.
It might not be what you would hope or wish,
Yet - to me - this more chirpy approach,
Is such a better way to mourn.

That is how it should be done.
It's my funeral, after all,
And, barring serious accidents,
I'll only get the one.

FRAGMENTAL

A single wave would seem to suffice,
But I wish I could hug everyone twice.

This lack of contact, I would wish to avoid,
Alas, it's a norm that can't be destroyed.

There's a pain in the lack of it I'd like to omit,
Why does it seem so awkward to be intimate?

I regret the people I have not hugged,
As I leave the weight of emotion unplugged.

That standard is what makes me relent,
Whilst off on their way they have went.

Sorrow exists for the people unseen,
Whilst people they have been.

MEMORY HOLE

Unmade,
Unsaid.
Forbidden,
Hidden.

Unfinished,
Diminished.
Forsaken,
Taken.

Bleep,
Asleep.
Overlooked,
Unhooked.

Such it was, from on high, dictated,
That all the prior be obliterated.

Have a nice day.

SHADE OF PURPLE 3: THE WORLD BEYOND

DECIPHER

There íqua em certain complexity,
Ene dae little-known majesty.
Odé other lexicons,
End their own hid dimensions.

Ene languages natural and constructed,
There íqua em thread twar bes conducted.
That might seem so simple end obvious,
But it íqua hard twar bes perfect for an audience.

Especially swen deí might noren grenes dae words,
Æ dae might efi Chronos ticks forwards.
Incomphrensible it may yar become,
But me live ene hope it may maden sense for some.

Swen there íqua common ground,
Ene those endings found.
Ieom may yar work ene reverse,
Twar coerce.

Beauty efi teft languages overlapping,
Ene subge careful mapping.
On em journey that exists pene time,
Twar understand dae perseverance efi rhyme.

BRICK WORK

Did you not notice? Pay attention
To the cracks and the
Scuff
Marks.

All which meet in their places
On every
Uneven ledge of the bricks
Before you.

Underneath the asymmetric sky
And beside the curved pavement
In those walls and halls
Of what sits here.

Because the Earth is of earth
With the people of people
And don't you know? People trip
On uneven pavements and the earth reaches up.

UNTIMED

Time that eyes of mine be thrown open,
so they might happen to see.

Not blind but lost,
in some past fantasy.

Clocks hum - no longer of a ticking sort,
but nonetheless, they move towards my hour.

My body onwards keels as the days continue,
for that Chronos does devour.

Felt in my now blinking eyes,
the passing sun in the skies.

Soon for the moon to take its place,
in the cold clear arrangement of space.

WORDS OF POWER

Do you know how
to win a nation?
Words that tend
to a causation.

Manifesto
built the same.
My party for them
but I'll find someone to blame.

I read the books
I turned the page
and I'll make way
for a new age.

But one can learn
only so much
before history
needs a personal touch.

Take it all in
Course through my skin
Power sets in
And I shall win.

What can you do?
You've been my fool.
Reading my words to
make your world cruel.

Just as it seems
you're just a means
in my grand scheme
to build my dream.

Because whilst you
have been reading,
I have been out there
lying and leading.

CONTRARY

We strive to have the good and the best
Yearn for all that is liberty,
But we often forget details of the past
And that so does lead to captivity.

For the tragedy is just that
And not so simply injust.
Even in treason, one can be sat
Believing they did what they must.

We fear change and mundane motions
Yet lay claim a new world
Seek sense yet dismiss many notions
As our thoughts are unfurled.

As they tell us the truth is a lie,
And we can no longer tell who is 'they'
Or any of the reasons why
That these are the words they say.

YOUR FIRST RULE

The elder expects it as though some given right,
As if there be some entitlement to.
Yet, they would deny it with all their might,
Of me as something rather untrue.

But they can look down upon my wisdom,
Call upon with condescending tone.
I will not yield to their vision of a kingdom,
As though their chair was a throne.

That chair at the front of the room,
From which the institution expects it all.
Which in its demands might just doom,
All from the day that they begin to crawl.

Its flaws and biases may demand respect,
Though make no mistake of the cracks in it.
I do not back away or will give in,
Not for this, in all meaning - not a bit.

Their frustrations are not something I desire,
For they are trapped in a need to comply.
But I, however, know when there is a need for fire,
And there is, in me, only my name by which to die.

I'll fight for the respect that should equalled,
And they need know that until then, it's their name.
For my blade of words shall not be dulled,
As their words shall not be put to me for blame.

I will not respect that which makes me speak false,
Not even here in some simple test.
Perhaps my analysis of things will have it faults,
But to find that out is my quest.

You can push me and rant about respect,
For I know it is a hollow stage effect.
You can tell me to wait until I am you,
But I will not respect until you respect me too.

Only by breaking that rule and standing my ground,
Even by holding to your name rather than honorific…
Might there be some system improvement found,
Then we will each respect another - how terrific.

HAIKU-SENRYŪ

Face on phone in bed,
A gentle remedy daily,
From life for things left...

LINES DRAWN

Stood upon the line in the sand
as they tore away
all there was
to be proud of in this land.

I do not blame the masses
for there were pawns
in the games
of some rich asses.

And here where we're free
to no longer remember
what was real or fake
in what we see.

Oh, how they tore apart the towns
to line their pockets full of money
like a pharaoh might have craved honey
as they ran a circus of clowns.

THE QUARTET

Conscience.
For the liars
There's no appeals.

Determination.
When your mind
Does the deals.

Wisdom.
Learning it all at that age
Taking you onto some new page.

Truth.

JOB'S WORTH

Sailor
with a voyage to sail.
Writer
who has scripted this tale.

Painter
adding the finest brush strokes.
Comedian
landing their newest jokes.

Sculptor
carving and creating a story in material.
Artist
who used unusual mediums like tea and cereal.

Magician
defying what seems possible in plain sight.
Acrobat
soaring through the sky in what seems like flight.

Doctor
pushing against the odds to save.
Firefighter
and the disasters they brave.

Janitor
cleaning up all the floors.
Receptionist
sorting all that admin of yours.

People
who are far more than just their professions.
Human
with their own words and expressions.

SHADE OF PURPLE 4: STAGEPLAY

REGIMENT

(Inspired by a production of the play "Black Watch")

The 43 in 1739,
Then 42 in 1751.
Yet still 3 in 1881,
And here they remain even now.

Rossco knows not of future or past,
Only where he was stationed last.
A man of Angus in home,
Yet his accent now does roam.

The interviewer gets a gentle Lithgae,
Or perhaps it's now more Embrae - but who's to say?
The sounds matter less than what is said,
By Rossco in this pub just after he's been fed.

His mates have plenty of their own to tell,
About how it weren't pretty or swell.
Cammy McG and Stewarty L with their own drinks,
Both of them willing to say what the other thinks.

Pints of Guinness, even though they were ready to run,
For this is no folly or simple entertaining piece of fun.
They did'nay want to dae this explaining,
But what other options were remaining?

Every Sunday in the pub, the survivors came,
And here this time - that interviewer with no name.
Stumbling on the heels of a young research lass,
Who had found them all - and they all wouldn't pass.

DEMETRIUS 1

(Inspired by an adapted performance of "A Midsummer Night's Dream")

Dimi was the boy who ran away,
Away from her on the wedding day.
His parents had called his bluff,
After years of him acting tough.

Held far from them, he'd felt cold,
And they seemed unchanging as they grew old.
From the youngest years,
They were apathetic to his tears.

His family were a sort traditional,
In a world that seemed so conditional.
Whilst around them, little Dimi would see,
That most of the people would not be.

It was young Dimi who set his mind,
To how he could be part of that kind.
But he could not find,
A way to become thus aligned.

Most other children would look at his clothes,
And it'd resemble nothing of what their parents chose.
For he was in the robes of time gone by,
And they were in sweaters and shirts spun anew.

They wrote prose, whilst he spoke poetry,
And in time, he tried to converse in that.
But it was a stumbling thing,
Even to - in a mirror - rehearse.

As he grew, he knew that he could not be,
So he settled for the books of the family library.
In those, he found tales of time,
To which there was indeed a rhyme.

Built himself upon the gilded gold,
Of those gone past folklores.
Wore his robes with all the appearance,
Of pride that they surely would have.

Still, it remained of little recompense to him,
Even as his knowledge and his vocabulary expanded.
For his friendships did not,
And what more was there to be had?

Cold winters would come and go,
But he would remain as the years turned.
Within his books, yearning to understand.
He came to understand much but not what he yearned.

With each new melting of the ice,
Growing older and wiser.
Yet forever frozen out from the others,
As the school years went on.

Dimi's words remained too poetical for most,
His attempts to be with the many cut him from the few.
By the Athenian light as it reflected,
In the English snow.

For came eventually a day to be wed,
Yet at the moment meant to be - he fled.
Unable to even look at the woman betrothed,
Now to him as though loathed.

Thusly, came the end of the April month,
And the nearing of the May Day.
Upon which the dew of the trees,
Might bring some light relief.

Caught for now in his tangle of gold-red,
Demetrius knew by what manner to pursue.
In the old man Egeus, he found a heart that chimed,
And - the first in many years - Demetrius smiled.

Sure it was that he would come to woo,
So he did until that wretched sunrise came to pass.
When Demetrius and Egeus found Hermia,
In the arms of one Lysander.

Off to the palace, the matter was hence rushed,
For in this, Egeus felt most needed.
Demetrius nodded in agreement,
Holding his sword at hand.

For in the days just past,
Demetrius had been given a gift.
Not by his father's glory but by Egeus' blessing,
In that Hermia's hand was to be taken by him.

At last, it could be that,
Dimi could feel the nearing warmth.
A rising sun of heart,
To be had in unification with Hermia.

But here had come that man in all his quiet calm,
Which seemed to Demetrius all frustrating.
His words in past had served all the same,
In that they thoroughly sought to admonish.

Lysander called him a hypocrite,
For turning his back on that Helena.
Lysander took him aside on one path,
Once telling him to contemplate his emotion.

All this, to Demetrius, was a simple trick,
For what would compell that man to care?
That Lysander, who like the rest, wore no robes,
Instead draped in merely a shirt and jeans.

Lysander, with shoes in need of careful tying,
And his hair needing to be so gently styled.
How could he dare to attempt supplanting
Demetrius, who had could barefoot walk miles?

This young lad, who like himself,
Seemed to be on a journey of life.
Yet would mock him for understanding where,
Hearts truly fell.

There was a spark lit there,
Between the two.
For this Lysander seemed so happy to have
Switched affections so sudden to sweet Hermia.

Red waves of rage coursed Demetrius,
In consideration of the greatest of Lysander's fouls.
He had given Hermia some crafted rhymes,
As though that was not thievery of Demetrius' ways.

His poetry was his life,
So he decided to best the man.
Switching for prose to fight Lysander's bewitching,
Making that the battlefield ahead.

Though he spoke as that invader bid,
His mind kept by the poetry as he did.
In Theseus' presence and palace,
He let Egeus recount Lysander's malice.

Clearly, he would let the elder take the floor,
To tell all of this faux-paramore.
Jarred, though, it did when Egeus told,
Of how Lysander had been so bold.

Even moreso than Demetrius had known,
Bracelets, rings, trifles, kites flown.
That clean-shaven interloper in pursuit,
Despite right by Egeus that was in no dispute.

For Theseus, in the finest poetry of the past,
Noted Demetrius' worthiness fast.
Tender struck Demetrius in that he could continued see,
Of Hermia and all that might be.

Such had this Lysander corrupted her,
That she was willing to die by the blade - that cur.
Or even to live away from either as nun,
A fate that to Demetrius seemed worthy of no one.

She was given a ultimatium - to relent and swoon,
By the time of the next new moon.
Upon Theseus and Hippolyta's wedding day,
Fast approaching as the start of May.

Demetrius demanded that Hermia see sense,
And that Lysander yield to his desires hence.
Lysander poured scornful response in turn,
Remark to marry Egeus seemed to make Demetrius burn.

EXCERPT FROM A LETTER TO JEFFY

(Adapted from a poem originally written in 2018 - as part of a 'personal prop' letter for a production of "RENT".)

Jeffy, my eternal heartbeat.
My heart every so heavy, darling,
longing for you - my ever so charming.
It was destiny that we meet.

Your eyes warmest brown,
smile lighting the sky on fire.
You gave me a feeling of which I'd never tire,
as we could perhaps, one day, walk the town.

Jeffy, my eternal heartbeat.
Girls most men only talk of,
but none compare to our love.
Forever waiting until we next meet.

SEVEN AND FIVE

(Inspired by an abridged performance of "Tally's Blood")

He liked you, you know.
That's why he'd come and sit with you
in your uncle's ginger store.

You didn't realise it.
Dealt with the games you put him through
and even tried to grin.

The day he came to you crying.
Because his dad was dead
is when he knew you would be around to the end.

And now, he's standing over there.
All these years on and he's said
that he wants you as more than a friend.

UPON MY NAME

(Inspired by an abridged performance of "The Crucible")

It comes as no surprise that it comes to nothing.

Her forgiveness will not help my soul for it is not my own.

They will not hear false confession from me for anything.

Or bear any false claim or witness upon my tongue.

I know that I am no saint yet they will not prise this from me.

Never shall it be nailed upon the doors of the land upon my name.

MICHAEL

Torn in two
Known to no one
Then to a few.

Bringing his might
As he continues his quest
For what he sees as right.

Partnered up in a way
That will lead towards
Some form of 'darkest day'.

Coated in emotions, but mostly brains
And never quite enough hearts
Though that's key to breaking the chains.

Nobody is ready for the day his rage shows
For he will stop at nothing to enact
The thing that nobody knows.

ON THE JOB

(Inspired by a production of "9 To 5")

Coffee smell
and wakening.

There, unfound,
would be you.

But there's no time
to wait.

For the boss needs me
on the job, and in time too.

You were the only thing
that ever got me through.

So now, handling the daily treadmill,
how will I last without you?

THE BARTENDER AND THE BODYGUARD

(Inspired by two roles in a performance of "Copacabana")

Catches him offguard
when the tall brute speaks
as though his brain
had never before thought it could occur.

The tan figure remains cold-faced
but even then
this feels out of
place.

Life at the bar meant few questions
and fewer answers to be given
else
one be found dead.

Here, however, was the man Luis
inquiring about more
than just a recommendation
of tipple for his boss.

Across the room, that boss sat
never quite out of Luis' sight
for that was the job
and it paid him well.

So, why then had he said more to him
than even his colleagues often would
as they rinsed out glasses
and took out drinks to tables.

He couldn't quite be sure
but for a moment, it seemed like
the gruffness melted away from Luis
letting a glimmer of a grin appear on his face.

"You seem a good man.", ended the conversation
from the bodyguard as he lifted a drink
for his boss
and yet he left behind his number on a card.

UNABRIDGED

The cold darkness outside the windows
feels miles away for the Captain
as around him - the flames burn.

Systems damage and unusual shapes
to the fire seems all
too erratic.

Cause, external but
Untraceable
in the dark.

Effecting procedures is the Captain's choice
and one not taken easily
yet he would wish nothing less for his crew than safety.

He has a sense of calm
as he always does
even as an engine is lost.

The crew and passengers are safely stowed
for their escape, and with a sigh,
he casts them off with a button press.

Alone
but for a yet-to-come
collision.

The ship goes down
and she gets closer to
striking.

Yet, he is the ship
and she is the
captain.

Bonded together and
destined
for this final stop.

They come into the planet's orbit
and as the ship tears piece
by piece - he feels the pain.

She has a sense of being asunder
mixed with the certainty
of his form for now.

His mind screams with the
fears of a doomed person
yet are somewhat quelled by the ship's duty to logic.

Together, as they make impact,
they are - ship and captain of the stars –
existent as one and then gone.

A FINAL BOW

(Inspired by a surprise short-notice appearance in 2019, as an unnamed ensemble character in a production of "Camp Rock: The Musical")

I never really wanted this job
And it was never about the kid's parents
Or the money being paid.

But here I was - doing someone a favour
By looking after their niece's whims
It must be said.

And somehow, I ended up having to help
More than that just that
When one of the staff was ill.

It was simple enough to carry the vote results
Within a lightly earmarked envelope
Carefully like it was someone's will.

Hand over, and in a moment that seems
Not quite anyone else's, it feels
Right to give a little spin.

Pirouette, and then to the crowd
I gave a bow to call the end of a simple little
One-time job that felt like a win.

SHADE OF PURPLE 5: THE WORLD INSIDE

UNTITLED

Nobody but me staring at blank page
Nothing in mind
No idea
Nothing new.

I look for the attention, crave it
Yet no word will do
For how can I word that which is
Yet to be found?

Here I am, linguistic suspension
Unable to ease that mind's tension
Slowly goes steadily numb
Unable to overcome.

I am silence
Wanting for words
And something new
My keys defunct
As I am too.

My head sprints so wild
Yet no word will do
But somehow in that trap, that aching cage
I have found some dimension
Of words to be put - upon the blank page

LIVERPUDLIAN B&M

I fell into a world where there was a B&M,
In Liverpool - but is that even true?
Down the aisles of a distanced land,
Searching for things from Doctor Who.

Is there a B&M in Liverpool?
I know not.
Is there a B&M in Liverpool?
It's a dream I never forgot.

In the morning hours, usually,
No bridge between me and there.
This came to say something to me,
Leaving a mystery I cannot bear.

Is there a B&M in Liverpool?
If so, the interior will not be as I saw.
Is there a B&M in Liverpool?
Yes, I know it's not some epic draw.

Things that didn't exist,
Except in this remnant of a could-have-been.
Querying things with a cashier,
Is hardly the most exciting dream I've seen.

Is there a B&M in Liverpool?
Why it stuck with me, I'll never know.
Is there a B&M in Liverpool?
Any future reality to what I found - I'd hope so.

In among the products,
With only the company of thy shelves.
A crowd wandering,
In hopes of, I presume, finding ourselves.

Is there a B&M in Liverpool?
The first fantasy I remembered waking in years.
Is there a B&M in Liverpool?
If not, then in that dreamland, better luck for my peers.

YOUR DAY TODAY

(Adapted from prose I have previously written called "Saturday 21st May 2022" - written on that titular date.)

If you had a bad day,
Read on, read on.

Because I know you've probably had a lot.
Yet I will never fully know what today, for you, brought.
But that's okay, because the point is not that, I say.
The point is that you've gotten through the day.

Maybe you coped well and now climb to a new pinnacle.
Maybe not and you're feeling a little cynical.
Maybe you're needing your friends to help pull you back.
To the surface, from the whirling rapids that attack.

But the point is you've reached the end of the day.
You have, and what a brilliant thing that always is, I say.
Whether you laughed, or cried, or have fallen in love.
Lost someone, smiled, angered, hurt, or all of the above.

In that day, that rotation, those hours.
You have managed today - that's one of your powers.

There is no shame in that, for that in itself,
Is a great achievement worthy of putting on your shelf.
Whether you've had a break day from strife,
Or the most productive day of your life.

You did today.
And no matter what they say,
That can never be taken away from who?
Yes, _____ can never be taken away from you.

Everyone you care about and love will always be proud,
Sure, they may not say it in blunt words and loud.
Perhaps in a look, or a smile, or a silly text, or some gift,
Or in even an invitation to go out, to give you a lift.

I did today - it hurt, and it warmed, I cried, and I smiled.
So many emotions that could be compiled.
Something tore in me, whilst another thing was patched.
Life's complexity forever unmatched.

And all I can say - all I know - at the end of a day like this,
Is I must let you know, keep you away from the abyss.
Yes, you, and you,
And you - no excuse.
And even you; the person who never believes
That you means you in a list of three yous.

Let you know that I am proud.
Yes, I am a rambler stubborn enough to say that loud.
Let you remember that you did today.
You can tell that it's all I am ever going to say.

Let you see - what you'll never fully know.
What I will try to show.
Perhaps you can have just a glimmer of that.
I can slip it in amongst the general chitchat.

That in my eyes, and my steps, and my speech,
What you are to me - perhaps that I can teach.
Because, you know, I've had a lot,
Yet you will never fully know - that, I've not forgot.

But that's okay.
The point is that I've gotten through the day.
And so have you.
That much is true.

BRONZE, SILVER, GOLD

If I were cast in bronze
All my hopes would be
That down it be torn.
For in flesh,
Bone, and blood
I happened to be born.

If they pulled it from its
Plinth,
You might think that I would wince.
Instead - if there be a soul,
I think it would question what once done
Had become known appalling since.

If you built me up upon that hill
That differs from a painting
Or even a photograph.
For you seek to carve me worship
When I am as equally capable flawed
As any other that served history's behalf.

If you see that I was of small quibbles
And faults not worth to mention,
Then I am satisified to win comparison.
But more than that - I simply would not need,
As anything more would transcend legacy
To become rather quite a warison.

If you must be rendering me in marble
Then I will marvel at your interest
But thus humbly request a simple one thing.
That it be seen as some fictional man
And not redressed as exact of me
For I am no god, no saint, no king.

If you will see it fit to press my head
Upon some silver coin,
Instead pass it to some other reputation.
For I would sooner see you get
The silver given to the poor,
In show of a generous caring nation.

If I were to be heard,
Awards in life and pictures of my times
Would be acceptable until my very end.
Sketch, paint, reflect my face then –
But never me upon a gold statue that places
Me above others - please do not pretend.

For in flesh,
Bone and blood,
I happened to live.
And for a legacy,
Only what I have said,
Should be what you can give.

BEACH

Embers on the wind, fated to ask me
if the birds like to be free
or if they, too, carry the weight
of shurking off the waves of hate.

Perhaps they hoist their hearts
in little broken parts
on chirping insecurities and fears
that reach only apathetic ears.

The wind rushes on
as the waves crash upon
the edge of the beach
in the places that most cannot reach.

TO BE

The pocket watch hangs
in the air,
between me and the mirror.

In both reflections - there are
many views of me,
threaded like the chain.

Have I ever been just one of them?
Perhaps I have been,
or maybe I've been none.

So much I could say
and so much they tell me,
of what they think I was.

I release my grip
so that the watch may let me slip away,
as it stays put.

DAYS, NIGHTS

Journey beckons
in self-discovery
I think I know.

Some afternoons you see
the smiling persistent man
who pushes you forwards.

Whilst nights hidden
convey the fatigued nihilist
from layer to layer, level to level.

In evenings, there is love
where in mornings - they've had enough.

Until Monday, there is them,
but the curse of Friday draws a line.

SANDS OF MIND

As I pirouette across the dusty
Sands
Seeking warmth in the faded
Emerald memories
I dance around the happy moments
Tread lightly on the darker
But they all make part of the Half-forgotten routine.

Glistening sun reflecting into yellow shades
Whilst I am made a fugitive of my mind
In time
Trusting
For there is no way back to re-experience
That moving shifting kaleidoscope
As I twirl my way
Across the dancing floor of dust.

You hide my life in watches, diaries and photos,
In love not malice
But it seems ever
More increasingly
Distant
Turning
Spinning
Twisting.

My feet claw through the sands
By the many grains
As I cross the plains of a
Unrememberable whole
And I build whatever
Sheltering sanctum I can from the
Chaos.

Some moves in the moment
Sluggish soup - wadding through treacle
Where others whoosh
Whip
Run so fast
Until their last
But in the end, all that they all are
Are moves to the melody of memory.

Photos burn in fire
Others swim in recognition and recollection
Tune fly through the air
Whilst I carry on choreography through the sand
A routine made of my past actions
Where I now miss some marks - or did I miss them then?
All I can do is play on through the symphony
Of the shadows of scenes seen in auld lang syne.

WILD BLUE YONDER

I was filled with wonder,
So for the first time,
We ran,
Whilst the lenses held us,
In their coloured focus,
As we shot past.

Rolling on as they ponder,
How two of us could roll and rhyme,
Man,
How they will discuss,
Even ask how it never broke us,
As we held onto until the last.

Shift, shape, and sort,
Ourselves anew,
Into the new generation,
Finding ourselves standing on a new rooftop,
And in the crystals of the stars above,
We find ourselves becoming the ones who fall upwards.

Never to stay in the expected scheme.

Or even to strictly subvert,
But where is life if not to be found
In the ways of change meeting tradition?

Don't know what's down there,
In the up-through-the-air.
Crowds will hope to find our tune,
Within the May Week of June.

Violin plays,
Crimson says,
Zesty days,
Woody ways.

Swimming swiftly through the aquamarine,
As it turns into goldenrod,
Yet somehow feels like the mightiest purple,
Of some new frame, some new scene.

Overmorrow is our destination,
And the land we left behind is in clear view,
Till, of course, we find ourselves with the stars.

Out there in the orange, and yellow, and white,
Leaving green lands behind, whilst the red,
Runs through us,
On our way forever,
Through the blue.

The land below tears asunder as do the stars.

Find ourselves unconfined
With nothing to separate
This from that
Or
There from here
As we tumble forth
Forever flowing
Unknowing
Rowing
Past Charon's sight and Oberon's might
Into the granted and well-virtued
Landscape
Of the wild blue yonder...

INAMORATO

Once we said we might fall together,
others did, and we thought there could be forever...

Time to say what will benefit neither of us,
for I hope life will take you somewhere good.
More than that still, I hope to all that exists,
that I changed you for the better in some slight way.

No need for snark or ill talk behind backs,
that's all I ever hoped as I fell from lust to guide.
You were the closest that the world ever gave
for that brief time, that must be said.

You are sure to be healthier without
me, and perhaps I too will be in absence of.

Find the part of you that smiled and laughed as
you wrote on my second-best shirt and third-best script.
Kill it.

Look where we keep leading each other
even across those gaps in time we travel.
It is simple that you needn't bother,
for all the two of us do is unravel.

I wish to spare you, and I will not commit
your words and emotions to the page.
For that is the
final courtesy.

I put the bullet in us, and I do that alone,
even as you would beg otherwise.
You wanted to love me six times over,
and kill me for half a dozen of the other times.

How has ever of us improved the other?
All I have ever been is the same things.
Can you see now what I have brought?
Things that others could have - and have - done.

If you need that, you need proper help.
If you need this, there are far more people.
If you need the other, then I have never been good at that.

Please.
Do not make your
will
disharmonious with the natural universe.

I wish you
some piece of salvation.
as I hoist your song aloft
and hope you will become a kinder person.

This, now, is not cold or callous,
nor is it done out of malice.
Just because you don't think it
doesn't mean it is untrue.

You should never remember me after this,
and I am sorry for I will not acknowledge you,
so no longer think of me in any such glowing light.

Prove yourself to be free of that one kiss,
then show me that what I think to be true,
and you can forget me past this night.

I must ask who you are, and so I will never know you.
You might ask who am I, and yet it will never matter.

SHADE OF PURPLE 6: LUST

THE APP

"Discreet now"
They don't want you to ask their names, why or how.
"Remember me from school?"
You're surely not thinking that this open is cool.

[Sub who never answered the general chat]
At least I can tell where you want to leave things at.
"FUN NOW?"
Finding urgency in the caps lock, that's how.

[Expires after one view]
Dreadful when alone, but intriguing when there's a few.
"Hi how'd you like someone like me to skull█████?"
I'm sorry but with my schedule, you'd be out of luck.

"What are you into?"
TV shows, languages and Ubuntu.
"No, I mean, what are you into?"
Evidently, you.

"Can you drive?"
Sorry, but joyriding ain't where I thrive.
"Swear u went to my school"
And you never thought of me as more than a fool.

[Easy (with a winking face)]
They all seem to demand a specific time and place.
"New to this, dress me up and show me a good time"
Maybe if I was still in my prime.

"Couple looking."
This'd be great, but I'd want to help with the cooking.
"Who's skint"
I'm afraid I'm not run solely by who has a mint.

"Please ruin me one day"
Uhm, how... kind of you to say?
[Big for (down arrow symbol)]
Fair play for keeping it simple.

"Looking for anything with anyone within reason"
In this place - what is there left to consider 'treason'?

AS DONE UNDER NEON

Running roaring
sweating soaring
through the air,
as it sweeps our hair.

Summer will surely end
but until then - let's pretend
that we can reason
with the turn of the season.

Blood, heat, sweat, trust,
in this coursing pulse
of our heartbeats
across the neon landscapes.

All that we were or are is together
in our gentle fight
through the darkest nights
as we strive for the middle.

We step into the spot of lights
and run the burnt orange pursuit
of our greatest hopes
whilst sprinting onwards.

They wish that they could catch up
but there is no way to chase a hookup.
Let's not hold back from where we intend
to go as we work to the journey's end.

ANOTHER FOLLY

Why did you have to play with things you didn't know?
Why did you have to risk reaping what you sow?
Powers that you didn't comprehend.

You felt a heat, not from passion or lust,
but from the dissolution of trust.
Burning through all of you, let's not pretend.

For so long, you did wonder,
and then came the day that you realised your blunder.
It was too late by then.

All in embittered tears and torn memories of past,
as you wish you could undo what you did last.
However, I am gone - into neverwhere and neverwhen.

GAME

Mountains of men would admit their miscalculations,
Even further admit when they've lost their games,
Of friendship, work, and love,
Yet few of lust.

Those are the rules of the play,
Whether by the alleyway or the bedroom,
And we all obey them,
As they bid us forwards.

The acceptance of lost love,
Pales in comparison to that,
Of the unfound lusts,
Which never get to run their course.

Play your game as you will,
But don't expect me on the horizon,
With my hands clutching to another,
In the afterglow of that sunset.

Because, let's be real, nobody wants to play,
With the talking dictionary,
Not even one that has some semblance,
Of good-fortuned looks.

We have lost the game, day after day,
Of running round the forest for a cherry,
And if that phrase does make some resemblance,
To a euphemism - then you've read enough books.

There is no shame in saying it,
When it is simply a simple truth,
And it is better to live openly by the simple things,
Than dishonestly within those, for that is a cage.

Lust is far more unforgiving than love,
For it takes away in two-word replies,
And clubs in the twilight hours,
Like you've never known elsewhere.

And you can never argue or reason with lust,
For you take your shot and that is that,
Yet if you lost,
Why is that much not admitted?

Join us in the corner that will speak truth,
Of how we have endlessly lost the game of lust,
As we drink ourselves around the next night,
And talk to each other of bygone fantasies.

Lost to burgeoning loves,
Lost to better looks,
Lost to not being the fit,
Lost to not finding the time or the place.

We have lost the game,
But in playing it and losing it,
We are, at least, as honest,
As we ever were with the other games.

WINE

Rhyme and rhythm
as I hear pitches and tones.
Deep in my mind
and running through my bones.

So much for doing unto others
as what they do to you.
Little hypocrisies
seem to be nothing new.

Welcome to the show,
let's leave those fools behind.
Because I can admit
that I ain't one of a kind.

Still be pouring,
just say when.
Don't go ignoring
words from my pen.

I don't need some shirt collar
paid for in gold.
Ain't here to shut up
and just do what I'm told.

Regardless of all that
I'm gonna shine.
Gonna do what I can
to make this show mine.

Do I keep going
and let your cup overfill?
Careful now, else
you'll find the crimson spill.

CUFF LINKS

There under the reddish light,
where you want to be bruised,
in that place underground where you're ███████d.

From the moment I tore off your shirt,
took off those glasses,
wandering hands wander ████s.

You ask for me,
tight on the ropes and chains,
wherein there is pleasure made of ████s.

Hair in hand and chin in the other,
as we're reflecting in the dimly lit mirror,
and I hear you ever ███████r.

You faintly utter your flights of fantasy,
and clear-cut desire,
not like someone for ███e.

Gently biting at that spot on your neck,
then with a little more force shown,
pursuing the path until there comes a ▮n.

Never using the time to escape,
except a moment to pull your rope,
and see if your head can ▮e.

Wanting me,
in turn I give you,
until knuckles turn ▮e.

Check your eyes to see your comfort,
even as your voice is lost,
no longer able to beg to be ▮d.

Marked, bruised,
didn't need to ask to be sucked,
so content to be ▮d.

Against the wall, as always, pressed,
hands on plums and arms round your chest,
along your lips, I run my thumb,
as in that last moment, from in chains, ▮m.

NAME UNSAID

When all I wanted was peace
clamoured on, they did, with jokes of ▬.
Seemed it'd never go away
as all they'd ever choose to say.

Hiding it in that hair was ▬,
a lad quite simply bonnie.
Hope fell piece by piece,
where others drew him - I cease.

Next came cute ▬
who didn't ken…
Until the reunion came
and for that, I don't blame.

What about that tall ▬?
On a cloud of wit, he blew in.
Knew what he was doing,
every little smirk he threw in.

Perhaps some hope for this gay
with the maestro ▮.
Songs of gold
but a side untold.

Few of you ever knew what came after
in life's next chapter.
Where there were idle thoughts of bliss
under raspberry skies with ▮.

And yet, not one of you was ever right
about who was the first 'beautiful sight'.
Never ever seeing behind the curtain of the past
to the first one in the list - of this unknowing cast.

But he
Was ▮.
Or, at least, that's what he was to me,
but I doubt any of you will ever see.

And many more yet still could be framed,
yet it was fanciful thoughts you have all famed.
In this humble little life's thread
of names left unsaid - yet somehow read.

UN/RAVEL

There is something rather quite
irresistible
about that moment when we're
entwined.

That join between our eyes as
you
are overwhelmed by that electric
surge.

In the moments where you are
unwound
and find yourself being rewrapped up in
me.

Between when I found you out there in the
pub
and then we tore on to the
club.

You knew what you wanted, so did
I
and now you are torn asunder with
me.

Until you are remade in one brief
second
for however casual this is, we have both been
reshaped.

(S)WORDS

Your hand on the hilt
At the stage of the swordplay
Where it felt like a slow hit
To my spine, with some little delay
As we raise our weapons bit by bit.

Gripping tighter
As we swing in motion
Getting lighter
Not in careful devotion
But swift desire.

Swords thrust forwards at speed
Battling to finish the other
Even drawn with marks that almost bleed
Striking another
Carefully, but in all depths of need.

WORDS

You arch back and the words slip
off your reddened open lips
from your opened mind
reveal to me - a stranger -
secret blown desires.

SHADE OF PURPLE 7: LOVE

SWIPE

A bare but crafted chest,
Swipe onwards.
Witty pun,
Swipe onwards.
Star sign held high in emoji,
Swipe onwards.
Pets and pictures thereof,
Swipe onwards.
Moodily lit selfies,
 Swipe onwards.
 Ages in variance,
 Swipe onwards.
 Years lived,
  Swipe onwards.
  Faces with their creases and brows,
 Swipe onwards.
  Animals cared for and nurtured,
 Swipe onwards.
  Beliefs in the world and life,
 Swipe onwards.
  A body they hold out for examination,
   Swipe onwards.

Dietary needs in their mandatory declarations,
Swipe onwards.
Gym photos that betray a routine,
Swipe onwards.
Photos with friends on cherished nights,
Swipe onwards.
People who have been around the town,
Swipe onwards.
People who are looking for their first date,
Swipe onwards.
People at the beginning of finding themselves,
Swipe onwards.
People who have lives to lead,
Swipe onwards.
Interests, politics, race,
Swipe onwards.
Uni, height, social media,
Swipe onwards.
Shards of existence,
Swipe onwards.
Mysteries of what their day today has been,
Swipe onwards.
Unknowable parts of them beyond grasp,
Swipe onwards.
The playlists, the nights out, the friends,
Swipe onwards.

The day after day after day of their life,
Swipe onwards.
That person who was born and survived and is here now,
Swipe onwards.
That person who had to torment themselves on form,
Swipe onwards.
That person who agonised their description,
Swipe onwards.
That person who struggles to let a piece of them be seen,
Swipe onwards.

Bad hair day, lost relative, trauma all unseen,
No room in the Swipe for all that they've been.
We swipe through remnants, footprints, echoes, ghost.
We swipe through fantasies - light imprints at most.

The Swipe never ends.

SWING

Did nobody ever tell you that?
That secret readying up to bat.
It takes eternities to get used to the swing,
if you can even come to make it your thing.

Love's never won or lost
like a game.
For all you'd hope they'd
say your name.

As those many colours fasten and flit
on the hopes of a base hit...
You find someone else has braced
to be the batter for the one you chased.

Yet it asks you to say some such
as it stabs your heart at a touch.
Ignorant of how the other brilliances
are not drowned by such experiences.

Have a scar that crosses your life
for all time
but patch up too as from out of this,
you will climb.

Up until the sunset's glow whether
one be alone
or in it together
carried by times yet unknown.

Before the end.
Never a game played with some bat.
For you will mend.
Did nobody ever tell you that?

GENTLE COULD HAVE

To remember from where you did spring
because there's where a heart dwelt upon.
Tender eyes trapping like a caged thing
in warm light there - then gone.

Under tree of bright oak and within
the tree branches borne of the cosmos.
Smile's nuance makes one lament sin,
as a future with you,
my mind stumbles across.

You court only a realm of modesty,
whilst I sink in mind of your lips.
A strawberry that pushes my honesty,
dream draw you to my heart and hips.

TO BE SPOKEN ALOUD IN AN EMPTY ROOM

I say "I love you" under my breath.
Even when you're not here,
That's funny, I guess.

TAKE THE WORLD

I could conquer the world with
just one hand
as long as
you are holding my other hand.

I could take the universe
as I command
so long as
you are aside me to stand.

SCENT

Your smell lingers in subtle ways,
In the tapestry of my begone days.
Beyond this realm where words take flight,
Our fragrances dance, pure and bright.

Breathe me in as I breathe you every time,
Scents forever to entwine.
A symphony of remaining scented dreams,
Unfolding onwards as time streams.

My essence lingers but wrapped in you,
Like rose petals kissed by the mountain dew.
I wish to keep your green coat and its scent allure,
Forever a blessing, and like you - forever pure.

KNOW

I yearn to know all about you,
Not just if you love me too.
Tell me about your day,
Even if it's not much to say.

Whether between the walls of your room,
Or in the wide expanse where flowers bloom.
Tell me of your dreams and hopes,
Your comforts and your nopes.

I'll soak it all up,
Like water to a buttercup.
For the finer brushstrokes of your life should put,
In my head as the picture of you takes root.

Talk to me about loves you lost,
Speak of what loving you will cost.
All the places you've been,
All the lovers your eyes have seen.

I want to hear of your jobs, and,
Your hobbies - it's what my mind demand.
In every finely painted detail of your life,
Is something to pull me past strife.

You're not boring or dumb or stupid,
Just afraid to tell nuances to Cupid.
Let me stay a while through the night,
To hear you gabble through what seems right.

Let me know the favourite theme tunes,
And if you like to run on the sandy dunes.
Do you worry about typing errors
On anthology tales of terrors?

Do you seek the attire
Of some character you admire?
Yearn for travel to faraway places
Or seek the wide-open spaces.

Are you looking for a couch to crash?
Seeking some quiet birthday bash?

Open up, please, to me,
So all of you, I can see.

And if I am the one, then there's nothing I need more,
Than for you to see that you, in whole, are not a bore.

You're more than your face and your eyes,
I love you beyond what you disguise.

Those little habits and needs you deliver,
Best to know all than just a sliver.

You are a person through and through in this time,
Let me know all beyond what can fit a rhyme.

All those careful edges,
Days running past hedges.

Let us, then, meet by the blooming flowers,
Of yourself - unconstrained as your soul towers.

Because, even if I don't fit the bill,
I've been here for you and always will.

CHERISH

I want to dance with you
whether in the sun
or the rain.

Oh, to whisper some shared
sweet nothings and
private jokes.

Sit with my arms around you,
run so swiftly in the horizon,
and hold you still in the blue.

Sloppy kisses on your lips.
Held glances into your eyes.
And secret words in your ears.

Ruffled hair,
gentle voice,
and all my tomorrows.

EMMET'S FAINT WORDS

Emmet faintly utters "I love him."
out loud
in a way that he's never done before
as though, for once, he's proud.

Less than a second later,
the muttered reply bristles in
with a "Shut the fuck up."
before joy can begin.

The most frustrating
senate
is the one of those voices
in the head of Emmet.

Fighting in a cycle of
hope and scolding,
about this affection
that he's beholding.

Must there always be
a reply
there to strike when he thinks
of this guy?

Emmet does it without thinking anymore
whilst he goes about his life
with "I love him" in weekly utterances
as the hour-hands cut time like a knife.

BEHIND BLUE EYES

Glistening smile
that never fails
to brighten up
- always prevails.

Undefinable.
How that pretty hair
sits so perfect from
the dawn to dusk there.

But most of all,
it's in those eyes.
The brightest navy
captures all the guys.

Your tongue gentle
as it, too, speaks.
Oh, that slight warmth
set on your cheeks.

Your hands yet gentler
for mine meant to hold.
Voice soothing comfort
as we brave the cold.

It's always those
eyes that take me.
Icy crystals – with
beauty there to see.

Behind sapphires are
wonderous worlds held
from the heights to the
low - I am compelled.

You slow me as I rush.
Hold me together as
I slip my hand to your
neck and the way I see...

Spots that are no imperfections
and such the brightest toothy smile.
My hand meets your neck so snuggly,
and I hold you tight for a while.

Because it all jumps and speeds up
around those blue eyes behind which
all men could be lost forever.
They seem to thoroughly bewitch.

I'd run away with you from the world
if only it be fair to deprive
the world of you and those brilliant bold
blue eyes that make me feel so alive.

Because there's so much beauty about you
in the smile, the voice, the hair, and that chest
but none of it ever quite compares to
the soul behind those blue eyes - that's the best.

AFTER THE SHADES

EPILOGUE

Once you've seen the droplets
purple
in their time,
you will never go back
to a world
without that shade.

The greatest quotes you can ever use
are the ones you create
for yourself
as it is only you
that can have that perspective
and voice.

But just you remember
that your brilliance expands
and stretches from the furthest star
up there in the sky
all the way down to the smallest grain of sand
on a beach.

ABOUT THE AUTHOR

Jamie H. Cowan

Jamie H. Cowan was born under a purple sky in a far-off place called Druimblaire (apparently, this place exists), in an equally far-off year. This book marks his debut as a poet. He began writing in 2011 and hasn't stopped since.

Outside poetry, Cowan has worked on fictional prose & several non-fiction reference guides.

The H. stands for Hamilton.

Printed in Great Britain
by Amazon